HOW TO MAKE CHILDREN LAUGH

Michael Rosen is a children's novelist and poet. He has written and edited over 200 books, including *We're Going on a Bear Hunt*, and served as Children's Laureate from 2007 to 2009. He presents the acclaimed programme about words and language 'Word of Mouth' on BBC Radio 4 and is Professor of Children's Literature at Goldsmiths, University of London. Michael lives in London with his family.

Other titles in the series:

How to Play the Piano James Rhodes

How to Count to Infinity Marcus du Sautoy

How to Draw Anything Scriberia

How to Understand E=mc² Christophe Galfard

How to Land a Plane Mark Vanhoenacker

How to Remember Everything Richard Wiseman

HOW TO
MAKE CHILDREN LAUGH

MICHAEL ROSEN

Quercus

First published in Great Britain in 2018 by

Quercus Editions Ltd
Carmelite House
50 Victoria Embankment
London EC4Y 0DZ

An Hachette UK company

A CIP catalogue record for this book is available
from the British Library

ISBN 978 1 78747 157 3

Jacket design by Setanta, www.setanta.es
Jacket illustration by David de las Heras
Author photograph by Historyworks

10 9 8 7 6 5 4 3 2

Text designed and typeset by CC Book Production
Printed and bound in Great Britain by Clays Ltd, St Ives plc

CONTENTS

Introduction   1

PART I
The Theory   5

PART II
The Practice   33

Conclusion   51

Introduction

Charlie Chaplin once said that to really laugh, you should take the things that you find painful and play with them.

We all love the sound of a child laughing. I have performed in front of children many, many times, and I always gauge how well a show is going by how they laugh. As I do my show, I'm listening to them laughing. The more they laugh, the better I perform, and the happier the whole room grows.

As you'll see in the following pages, making children laugh isn't terribly difficult. You just have to understand where the laughter is coming from, and why it's necessary in a child's development. I'm no scientist, neurologist or psychologist, but I know it helps them find their way in life.

1

It's well known that if you pull humour apart you can kill it stone dead – but I'm going to risk a bit of dissection in the hope that my personal angle into what tickles kids will help you create enough laughter to make some rooms grow happy!

PART I

The Theory

'What's brown and sticky?'
'A stick.'

How does this joke work, and why is it so popular with children who hear it and then can't resist repeating it to each other all the time?

There are two main triggers.

The first is that the joke appears to be talking about poo, and children love breaking the poo taboo. Poo is disgusting, intriguing and fascinating – what's not to like? It's a complex subject for kids for several reasons at once: they've been taught not to do it in their pants (that's what babies do, and nobody wants to be a baby); they've been told it's not polite to talk about it; adults seem to spend an awful lot of time and energy cleaning it away and hiding the smell of it. There's a lot for them to unravel here.

The second is that the person telling the joke isn't actually talking about poo. As we find out in their answer, they're talking about a stick. The comeback plays with the idea that both the joke-teller and the listener are thinking that the answer should, by rights, be poo.

At the heart of all this is anxiety: anxiety about behaving like a baby, anxiety about the unexpected, anxiety about appearing stupid. This particular emotion – anxiety – is a key motor for a good deal of humour. Let's look at this theory more closely.

There is no intrinsic reason for poo in itself to be funny. For that matter, we can widen the net so that it includes bodily functions that are appropriate for children, and the words for those functions: weeing, farting, burping, puking – even, if you tell the joke right, bleeding. In isolation, these natural biological activities just don't make you laugh.

It used to be that you wouldn't find references to such physical processes so much in children's books, but now they're easy to find. Think of the BFG 'whizzpopping' in front of the Queen in Roald Dahl's *The BFG*; Tony Ross's

6

I Want My Potty, in which the Little Princess comes to terms with forgoing nappies; Dav Pilkey's *Captain Underpants* books, with wild excessive descriptions of all things loo-related (one of the titles, *Captain Underpants and the Tyrannical Retaliation of the Turbo Toilet 2000*, says it all, really). And have you come across the extraordinary *The Story of the Little Mole Who Knew it Was None of His Business* by Werner Holzwarth, with its illustrations by Wolf Erlbruch of a mole with a turd on its head? Suddenly, in the right context, bodily functions become funny.

(Having said that, in some countries children have been laughing at such things in books for centuries, as in the German Till Eulenspiegel stories which I adapted as *The Wicked Tricks of Till Owlyglass*. All you need to know at this point is that it includes a climactic bum-kissing joke which saves the trickster Till's life.)

The reason bodily functions are funny is because they are surrounded by hundreds of rules of the 'dos and don'ts' variety. Part of what psychologists call 'socialisation' is instilling these 'dos and don'ts' into children so that they fit the norms that any given society thinks right: don't wee in your pants, do blow your nose, don't burp at the table etc . . . Children live in a world they haven't created and have very little control over. For a good deal of their lives, grown-ups – sometimes well-intentioned, sometimes not so – exert authority over them, telling them what to do, what not to do, where to go, when to come back and so on.

Children are therefore often anxious about whether they're saying or doing the wrong thing. If you have a character breaking a bodily function taboo, you shouldn't make it pathetic or sad, because it won't be funny. Truly pathetic or sad scenes bring out sympathy in us, and sympathy doesn't usually make us laugh. Think of, say, a child begging in the street, or how you'd react to someone breaking their arm.

Ideally, as we have seen with the poo/stick joke, there should be an element of the unexpected about it. The surprise that the stick joke works derives from the fact that there is an obvious answer to the question (poo) which is thrown out when the answer comes as something so ordinary (stick) that it's an unforeseen revelation. It also breaks an unwritten rule in jokes of the 'Question and Answer' kind: you don't usually repeat a word in the answer that comes from the question. Under normal circumstances that would be a not-very-good joke. On this occasion, it works because it is both obvious and not very good. And, again, this is unexpected.

8

Rule number one: surprise is always the most useful and reliable tool in your comedy toolbox.

It's not just bodily functions that entertain children thanks to their extreme naughtiness potential. There is a whole range of humour that works by having characters who are 'bad', not in the sense of being 'evil' but in the sense of being disobedient, subversive, rebellious and divergent; characters who don't do as they're told, who talk back to authority figures, or who plot and plan stuff that authority figures don't like. Think of Matilda's bleaching of her father's hair in Roald Dahl's book of that name; Danny and his father feeding sleeping pills to property baron Mr Victor Hazell's pheasants in *Danny the Champion of the World*, also by Dahl; the *Horrid Henry* books by Francesca Simon, in which Henry plays pranks on his perfect brother despite their parents' fury; the *Pippi Longstocking* books by Astrid Lindgren, where our red-haired and freckled heroine disobeys rules; or, going back some time, think of Toad in court talking back to the judge in the court scene in *The Wind in the Willows* or the dramatised version, *Toad of Toad Hall*. What happens in these examples is that they enable the child-reader to live out the fantasy of doing the subversive, rebellious, divergent stuff without actually doing it themselves and having to face the dangers of punishment that, in real life, would follow their rebellions. There may also be a dash of feeling superior to the 'bad' child caught up in that too.

Children often respond well to jokes that give them a sense of superiority. In the poo/stick joke, because the person telling the joke is talking about a stick, not poo, they are superior to the person listening to the joke. The answer sounds at first as if it's come from someone who isn't as clever as you, the listener – he or she is coming across as a person who would never associate 'brown' and 'sticky' with poo, whereas you have immediately made that connection. Many jokes work if they seem to flatter the person hearing it, with either the teller of the joke or the person in the joke appearing to be foolish in some way or another. The twist in this particular joke, though, is that the person telling it says something that sounds foolish but because it's caught the listener out, that person comes over as more sophisticated! This makes it ideal to pass on: you get cleverer by telling it.

Again, this all ties in with anxiety – anxiety about feeling like a baby, anxiety about not belonging, anxiety about being left behind.

10

And the reason why tapping into children's anxieties is so effective is because the humour produces relief. Rule number two: relief is a crucial part of humour. If we think of anxiety as being a full bladder that we can't admit to, then laughter is the moment when you can get to a loo and have a pee. It's the release of the anxiety-bubble. The exploding of a taboo subject, getting over a surprising twist or someone behaving badly getting their comeuppance all generate relief, and we express that emotion through the physical act of laughter. Part of comic technique is to fill the bladder with as much tension as you can. So, if you are writing about an authority figure, you can delay for as long as possible the time of their downfall for maximum effect. Think of Miss Trunchbull in Roald Dahl's *Matilda*, who is ridiculed and chased from the school thanks to Matilda's telekinesis powers, but only at the end of the novel.

Comedy will often emerge in these situations if the people being not-good are unaware of just how divergent they are being; they are 'vainglorious', i.e. full of grandiose ideas beyond their reach, the consequences of their actions resulting in pompous, nasty, overly pernickety behaviour. When these big-heads get their comeuppance in some undignified way, that's where you get the loudest laugh. An example from my own work (if I may) comes over and over again in my *Uncle Gobb* books. Here I have an overbearing uncle constantly demanding that his nephew answer general knowledge questions and do exactly what he says about eating and behaving properly. So he sees his nephew, Malcolm, eating his baked beans by putting the toast on top of the beans. The uncle protests and says to Malcolm's mother, 'But it's beans ON toast, not under the toast.' How can a writer undermine this kind of bossy behaviour? I made Malcolm's mother patronise Uncle Gobb, and so the moment he gets really obnoxious like this, she says to him things like, 'Oh, Derek, be a dear, pop round the corner to the shop, we've run out of milk.' And off he goes, very meekly. It's a form of 'bathos', the ancient Greek word for undercutting or undermining moments of tension with something earthy, or very ordinary. Uncle Gobb suddenly becomes a pathetic figure, which makes the situation funny.

Similarly, if the main character is the divergent one (e.g. the naughty child), then the longer the subversive activity or words go on the more dangerous it becomes, and so the comedic relief will be all the greater. Some humorous writing for children works on the idea that the divergent child character is constantly naughty but also constantly punished (think of Dennis the Menace in the *Beano* comic or, once again, Horrid Henry). The laughter comes from the fact that the 'bad' child is irrepressible. No matter what is said or done to that child, it makes no difference. He or she will be back next week, or in the next chapter, or next book, up to another trick, another escapade, another misadventure. What happens here is that this enables the child-reader to feel just that bit superior – that welcome emotion again – to the 'bad' child because the child-reader would not be so foolish to keep on behaving like this. The relief comes from the fact that the 'bad' child is in a sense doing the bad stuff that the child-reader half wishes that he or she could do – one natural consequence of all that authority that we adults impose on children is that it gives children the desire to want it to stop, to magic it away. Stories become comic when they 'give' children that magic. Imagine doing what Henry does and stitching up your goody-two-shoes annoying little brother all the time, or firing your catapult like Dennis the Menace whenever you feel like it.

Many of my true-life poems and stories turn on this. Take 'The Project', for example.

The Project

At school
we were doing a
'project'.

You know the sort of thing:
THE VIKINGS
TRANSPORT
WOOD.

Our project was:
HOLLAND.

There we were reading:
MY FRIEND HANS FROM HOLLAND
and we made: Windmills
and we stuck blue strips of paper
onto white strips of paper.
There were: Canals
And we kept talking about: Tulips
and: Cheese.
In the end,

I thought they grew cheese
and ate tulips.

Then one day
our teacher – Miss Goodall
said that there was an:
Inspector
coming in.
She said he wasn't going to inspect us.
He was going to inspect her.
And we were all to help her
by being 'really good'
and answering all the questions
he asked . . . us.

Later that day, he came in.
He had a moustache.
We behaved.
Miss Goodall behaved.
There we were, all sitting in our rows
behind our desks
breathing very very quietly.
And he looked at our: Windmills

and our: Canals
and he said:
'What do they eat in Holland?'
and I didn't put my hand up
in case I said: 'Tulips',
but Sheena Maclean said, 'Cheese.'
And he said:
'What do they grow in Holland?'
and I didn't put my hand up
for that one either
but Margot Vane said, 'Tulips.'

And he asked some more questions
and we were doing . . . 'really well'.
Miss Goodall was trying very hard
not to look proud
and then he asked:
'Who is the Queen of Holland?'

There was silence.

No one knew who was the Queen of Holland.

Miss Goodall frowned
and started looking all round the class
with her eyes looking all hoping.

Then suddenly I remembered this little rhyme
that my friend Harrybo used to say.
I put up my hand.

'Yes?' said the Inspector.

'Queen Juliana
is a fat banana,'
I said.

Miss Goodall looked awful.
Harrybo was sitting in front of me
and I saw him snort, and start giggling.

'What did you say?' said the Inspector.
'Queen Juliana,' I said.
'Good,' he said, 'you're right. Quite right.'
Miss Goodall was delighted.
I was delighted.

The Inspector was delighted.
And Harrybo was still snorting away
like mad.

Here you have the pernickety inspector lording it over a class of kids, and with the tension building after his question about the Queen of Holland's name hangs in the air, until a child (yours truly) says something from the child's world, not the education world, and it undermines and deflates everything. The child has crossed a line, the inspector is undermined, and the result, at the end of the poem when everything is resolved, is like one big respite.

Or there's 'The Noise', with my brother imitating the way my dad tries to keep us quiet even to the point of doing it right in front of him:

The Noise

If my father wanted you to be quiet,
he didn't say, shhh,
he didn't say, be quiet,
he didn't say, shuttup.

All he did was put his hand up
to the side of his face
and say in a quiet voice
that sounded as if
there was some kind of terrible pain
in the middle of his brain:
'The noi-i-i-i-se!'
It was as if the palm of his hand
was trying to reach inside
his head to get at some awful thing in there.

So, we would be going on a car trip,
Dad driving, Mum next to him.
Me and my brother in the back.
My brother says,
'There's an imaginary line
down the middle of the back seat.
I'm this side.
You're that side.
You can't cross the line.
I'm this side of the line.
You're that side of the line.
So –'

'Yeah, I get the point,' I say,
'there's a line.'
'. . . and you can't cross the line,' he says.
So I say,
'Yeah yeah, I get the point.
I won't cross the line.'
And I stick my hand over the line.
'Hey,' he says, 'you crossed the line.'
'I didn't,' I say, and I stick my hand
across the line again.
'YOU CROSSED THE LINE!' he says,
'I DIDN'T,' I say, and I stick my hand
across the line again,
'MUM! HE CROSSED THE LINE!'
'I DIDN'T,' I say.

And my dad's hand goes up
to the side of his face and:
'The noi-i-i-i-se!'

My brother used to imitate it.

If I was making a racket,
my brother would walk around the house
saying,
'THE NOISE! THE NOISE!'

So it's breakfast.
My dad couldn't stand any noise
at breakfast.
One sniff
and it was the GLARE.

He comes downstairs,
sits down in the chair
and opens up the newspaper.
You can't see him.
He's disappeared.
One moment you've got a dad
and the next you've got a newspaper.

All you see is his hand.
It comes out from behind the newspaper,
moves across the table all on its own,
finds the cup of coffee

and disappears behind the newspaper.
He didn't even drop the newspaper
to see where the cup was.
He just knew where it was.
We used to stare at the hand
coming out, grabbing the cup,
disappearing behind the paper.

Once, my brother
moved the coffee cup.
The hand came out,
couldn't find the cup.
The newspaper came down.
'What's going on?' says my dad.
He grabs the cup
and disappears again behind the paper.

Once, I sat there and a little voice inside me said,
'Hey, why don't you practise playing drums
on the side of the table?'
And I said, 'No, that would be crazy.
Dad can't stand any noise at breakfast.'
And the voice said,

'Yeah, but you know you want to.
Go on. Pick up the knife and fork
and blam blam blam, away you go.'
'No, no, no, I couldn't.'

But I did.
Knife, fork, side of table and
blam blam blam!

The newspaper came down
and my dad's hand went up to the side of his face.
He started to say, 'The no-i—'
But my brother was in there quick
with
'THE NOISE!!!!'

And my dad was left there with his
hand in mid-air still trying to say,
'The no-i-i-i-i-ise!'

When I perform these poems, I become the channel
through which the children can, for a moment, let go of
their anxieties about the authority figures in their lives. As

I'm performing these in schools, and as the children laugh, I can physically feel that relief across the divide between me and them. What's fun for me personally at that moment is that I know (of course) that I'm an adult and a parent in real life, but in the story I'm often acting out the divergent child. For some children that added layer of incongruity is another source of the humour. Again, the unexpected is always a good pump-primer for laughter.

We've looked at anxiety and relief as two main foundations of comedy. There is another one that lies in absurdities – rule number three – which often goes hand in hand with anxiety and relief. This introduces us to the use of exaggeration, another very useful technique. You can have a blast when it comes to the human body here, but only if you exaggerate the mishaps that can happen to bodies to such a point as to be unrealistic, giving us legitimate, non-discriminatory forms of comedy.

This is crucial: it has to be non-discriminatory. Society spends vast amounts of time and money worshipping the human body. It creates ideals and norms for what the body should look like. These are projected onto us as body types we're meant to conform to but also in terms of what things we wrap our bodies in (clothes, shoes), and how we adorn them (make-up, hairstyles). All this can be a source of deep anxiety: am I tall enough, short enough, thin enough, beautiful enough? Are the various parts of my body in the right place, the right shape? Are my clothes sufficiently smart and fashionable? Every aspect of this is full of comic potential because of the anxiety factor.

But we have to think very carefully about whether we're empowering children or ending up handing ammunition to bullies when highlighting physical traits or characteristics, however exaggerated. As we all know and often witness, verbal and physical bullies pick on those seen as diverging from the norm in even the tiniest ways, especially when it comes to body shape, facial ideal, appropriate clothes and the like. Even worse, if the norm is, say, being male, or being white, or heterosexual, then the bullying can be incredibly cruel to females, people of colour, gay people and so on. It's dead easy to join in with this bullying and mock characters just as the bully in the playground might. It may well produce laughs. Anyone interested in comedy has to think this stuff through.

With children there is the added complication that you must assume that most children under the age of ten (and some older) will not 'get' irony, if that's what you dress it up as. All this means that we have to tread carefully if we want our humour to be responsible.

Back to exaggeration . . . What's also good about it is that it ties into another area of anxiety: illness, accidents and death. Anything to do with parts of the body or a whole body suddenly and unrealistically shrinking, growing, falling off, having bits added onto it, exploding, miraculously transforming into parts or the whole of an animal, monster or alien – are all potentially full of comedy. Edward Lear's 'Dong with the Luminous Nose' is an early example, and the same goes for the baby turning into a pig in Lewis Carroll's *Alice's Adventures in Wonderland*. Roald Dahl's *George's Marvellous Medicine* has a good deal of bodily distortion going on, and a good few limericks work this way:

> There once was a farmer from Leeds,
> Who swallowed a packet of seeds.
> It soon came to pass,
> He was covered with grass,
> But has all the tomatoes he needs.

Or:

> An elderly man called Keith,
> Mislaid his set of false teeth.
> They'd been laid on a chair,
> He'd forgot they were there,
> Sat down, and was bitten beneath.

As I say, the less credible, the 'safer' the comedy is from any moral minefield. Don't hesitate to introduce further elements of incongruity, such as dragons or robots wearing clothes, say. Have a blast! It's not often as adults we give ourselves permission to wade into this alternate universe of craziness. Laughing is good for grown-ups too . . .

Another area rich for pickings with regard to absurdities is language. Children are surrounded by language that they themselves have not produced, from books to school rules, TV shows to parents' instructions. All this amounts to, in its own way, a huge body of 'authority' (yes, back to that chestnut – it's amazing how much this is linked to children's social and emotional development). Most children perceive language to be more powerful than they are, and so it becomes a source of anxiety again. They worry about mistakes, failure to live up to expectation, the consequences of getting it wrong, or of not understanding it. The most extreme version of this is, of course, tests and exams – set by mysterious unseen people, backed up by the authority figures of teachers, with parents clearly nervous about the outcome. This is why the whole area of the adult output of language, whether it's speech or writing, is ripe for parody. We know that children themselves make up parodies of Christmas carols, adverts and pop songs. Do you remember how as a child you would adapt school songs, hymns, prayers, school rules and sermons to get a few laughs?

We Three Kings

We three Kings of Orient are
Playing our electric guitars
One overloaded and exploded
Blowing us all afar.

Jingle bells
Batman smells
Robin's done a fart
The Batmobile's lost a wheel
And now it's falling apart.

28

I am particularly fond of this adaptation of the song from the animation film *The Snowman* by Raymond Briggs:

I'm flying in the air.
I lost my underwear.
I went to Mothercare
To buy another pair.

There is a canon of famous funny poetry, song and non-sense, going back to Shakespeare (remember King Lear's Fool blurting out fragments of nonsense), and the originators of funny poetry for children – Edward Lear with his limericks and absurd ballads, Lewis Carroll with his parodies and Hilaire Belloc with his ironic cautionary verses. There is also the tradition of the nursery rhyme: short snappy stories using a rollicking rhythm and rhyme system. Think of, say, 'The Grand Old Duke of York' which contrasts the grandiose figure of a great Duke and the pointless, repetitive activity of going up and down a hill. Or 'It's raining, it's pouring / the old man's snoring / he went to bed and bumped his head / and couldn't get up in the morning'. Some of this material works on the fact that rhythm and rhyme set up expectations, building to the concluding rhyming word of any sequence, be that a couplet (two lines that rhyme) or 'quatrain' (the classic four-line ballad form), the limerick (class five-line scheme), and so on. Ideally, you should aim for the main gag to happen on the last word so that the laugh comes after the end of the rhyming word, the whole short poem or a particular verse.

Pulling together the themes here, then, we have anxiety, surprise, absurdity and language-play all offering us a rich source for humour. Remember: keep in your head the idea of 'continuity and variation'. That means, build on what's out there, what you know, what you've seen makes children laugh, and rework it. Experiment by moving things around, putting in new words, introducing slightly different characters and putting them in slightly different situations. This way you use the known traditions of what will work, while creating something that feels and sounds a bit new.

PART II

The Practice

If you want to make children laugh, the best place to start is to remember what it was that used to make you explode with laughter when you were little. Regress a little! Think back to those jokes, songs, rhymes, facial expressions and body moves. What amused you then will inevitably be the kind of humour that you will be most able to perform yourself.

Start with the comedians in films and TV programmes you used to watch that made you laugh. When I was a boy, I loved a character called Mr Pastry played by an actor called Richard Hearne. These were slapstick films, with Mr Pastry ending up covered in whatever he was supposed to be working with. The gag was that he would start off with the best of intentions but then would show himself to be useless at it – that's a situation that many children have experienced, so Mr Pastry relieved me of feeling like a klutz. He was also an adult (of a kind) so it was extra funny because he was a grown-up doing what I, as a child, might have done. I also loved the Billy Bunter stories when they came out on TV, which worked a good deal of the time on the boy, Bunter, being defeated by his own greed and selfishness. One of the great comic actors of my childhood and teenage years was Phil Silvers, who played the part of Sergeant Bilko. If you want to see how a seemingly 'realistic' bit of acting is, in fact, a form of ancient clowning, take a look at some clips on YouTube. His gestures and facial expressions are all enlarged and exaggerated in the style of classic clowns. I adored his style when I was in my teens, and I know that sometimes I'm imitating some of his moves and expressions.

If you study people like these, you'll find that your voice, face and body have remembered the rhythm, timing and tone of those jokes from your childhood. Solemn and laborious though it sounds, it's worth making lists of these. Many of the greatest clowns and comedians have been students of the art, filling notebooks with gags, memories, tricks, rhymes and the like.

Now add to your list real people in your family, at school or in any kind of youth club you belonged to who said funny things or got themselves caught up in comical situations that amused you. Think in particular of those characters who had distinctive ways of talking. Recall their gestures and facial expressions, even their body shapes. I did this with my dad in particular, who had all sorts of gestures which seemed to come from another time. If he was amazed by something, he would stroke his hair back from his forehead in a tense sort of a way, while saying 'Extraordinary! Extraordinary!' Another one was when he wanted to say he was fed up with one of us: he used to tut, followed straight after by a guttural sound, a bit like a long version of the last 'ch' in the way Scots people say 'loch': 'chhhhh'. My brother and I loved imitating him: 'Extraordinary!' Or telling them about my father doing the 'Tut! Chhhhh!' thing and getting them to do them too.

Think of things that you and other children did around you at school that made you all laugh. I was lucky enough to be friends with several kids who could do what you might call 'mini-impressions'. They could pick a gesture or a single expression copied from a teacher or relative and this made the rest of us laugh. I even had a friend who could, in one second, perform the way Louis Armstrong would get out a hankie at the end of one of his songs or jazz solos and pat his head while smiling and giving out a little growly-squeaky sound. He just 'caught' it.

Another thing we 'got into' was a TV series that ran at the time based on H.G. Wells's *Invisible Man*. In each episode, the Invisible Man would either beat up someone, tie them up, or even bundle them into the boot of the car. But of course, you couldn't see the Invisible Man, so the person being attacked by him would have to mime being beaten up by someone who wasn't visibly there. We loved this and spent hours trying to replicate these fights. It was in its own way good mimed comedy and we would compete with each other as to who could be the best at tripping ourselves up, spinning round, pretending to be reeling from a punch on the chin, and so on. I've never forgotten this and it's built into some of the physical comedy I do.

You could make a note of equivalent stuff from when you were at school.

All this is your core comic material. What you're doing here is 'harvesting' what is already in your head and in your body. It's already in you, part of you, and it's what will come most easily to you if you're performing funny material as a grown-up for children. It's also helping you remember what is funny to a child, something that becomes harder to grasp as we become adults.

Next step: ask yourself why and how this stuff was funny to you as a kid. You may find my 'anxiety' theory helpful here. Was there anything in the gags and comic situations that touched on hidden concerns or fears, no matter how trivial or silly they might appear to you as an adult? Think back to what situations made you anxious when you were little – especially the ones that you didn't want to admit to other people. Come up with your own theories about why or how the material you loved used to tickle you.

The next thing to do is to look at what is making children laugh out there right now. This means spying on children's viewing and reading habits. The best way to do this is by watching those comedians and performers who do live shows at children's parties, in theatres or at literary festivals. There is really no substitute for this. You have to find out and learn from what's going down out there! And it has to be about what makes children laugh, not necessarily you – it's always the child audience that counts. Just because there's a book or a show that you think is funny, that isn't necessarily what's going to entertain those children around you. I've sat with my children on a good few occasions watching TV programmes that are supposed to be funny but I was the only one laughing. You need to find out what makes *them* chuckle.

This is vital if you want to write new material. As you take it all in, let your mind go off in creative ways as you come up with analogous stuff. Don't lose these thoughts. Jot them down. So, let's say you're reading David Walliams's or David Baddiel's books, or one of the *Captain Underpants* books to a child. As you read, let your mind make up similar scenarios, similar ways of talking, similar characters. There's no need to feel guilty about this. All writing and storytelling builds on the stories that came before.

Because that is exactly what you are going to do. You're going to explore those thoughts, and then play them around in your mind and inevitably reinvent them with points of difference – the outcome might vary, for example, or a context might differ. It's really important to be as free as you can about this. You can swap humans with animals, or the Romans with aliens in a futuristic setting. Or try mixing it up with Romans in a futuristic setting, with aliens and dinosaurs. Go mad! Go to extremes!

These two practical steps to being funny will serve you as well or better than anything else. The more you are a student of the material from your own childhood and the material that is out there now, the better a comedic performer or writer you will be. What you're doing is getting this stuff into you so that you're better at getting it out of you.

Indeed, as soon as you can and while it's still fresh in your mind, start using some of this content with children. Whether it's cracking jokes, singing silly songs, reciting funny poems or telling real-life stories, just give it a go.

What is of key importance here is that the moment you start storytelling and performing with real children, you start to read their faces, hear their laughter (or lack of it!) and it will affect what you say and how you say it. I can't emphasise enough how much this matters: you must, must, must listen to and watch your audience all the time. You may well look like you are 'being yourself', regardless of your environment, but in fact it's vital that your seemingly self-contained demeanour is a disguise, behind which you can spy on your audience, whether that's one person or five hundred people. I can't tell you how many performers I've seen who are less funny than they could be because they are not watching and listening to their audience. At the end of the day – it goes without saying – nothing is funny until someone laughs: no matter how hilarious you think your stuff is, it's not funny until you've got those kids laughing.

Apply what we've learned so far to your material. Remember the element of surprise and absurdity. It's worth going over comic material like, say, a Roald Dahl book, and finding the surprise elements that worked with children. The shock, horror and humour that comes from, say, *George's Marvellous Medicine* or *The Twits*. Yes! George really does come up with potions that can transform someone. *The Twits* really are more disgusting than anyone you've ever met!

We looked at the theory of why language can make kids laugh. If you want your humour to make full use of this, it's worth spending some time making a list of phrases that are familiar to children; maybe they've come from a particular TV series, adverts or the latest songs they've heard, or maybe they've emerged from the typical things that parents and teachers say when they tell children off. Change a few of the words round or leave words out to make what is being said ridiculous. You can subtly replace words with others that sound similar but mean crazy or absurdly different or taboo-breaking things. Think about puns, too! Children love them. Most of the puns in children's jokes derive from the 'right' one, or that it's not doing what words are supposed to do, which is refer to an object, process or name in the correct way.

'What's the strongest shellfish?'
'Mussels.'

'Doctor, doctor, help! I'm getting shorter and shorter.'
'Just wait there and be a little patient.'

In my book, *Barking for Bagels*, Shnipp the Dog tells the story. It begins: 'My name is Shnipp. I am a dog. This is my story. A dog's story. Shnipp's story. It's the truth, the whole truth and nothing but the truth.' Then there's a big picture of Shnipp's face (done by Tony Ross) with his mouth open with one prominent tooth sticking out. The story goes on: 'By the way, this is my tooth, the whole tooth, and nothing but the tooth . . .'

You can put the words of an original phrase, song or saying into the mouth of someone or something inappropriate such as an animal, a fruit, a tree, a robot or an alien that makes the words sound absurd. Or an inanimate object such as a coloured crayon (*The Day the Crayons Quit* by Drew Daywalt springs to mind). The fact that they transform into humanoid beings that talk and act as if they are people with the same kind of worries and concerns that we have is a source of humour, because of the absurdity of it all, as well as a relief

– these objects can give voice to the very things that bother us while making them funny thanks to the juxtaposition. And the more solemn or the more revered the original, the funnier the parody becomes. That's because solemnity and reverence make us anxious – will I be solemn and reverent enough? By making the authority that lies behind the solemn or serious words seem ridiculous, we feel reassured.

Obviously, a lot depends on your delivery, and how you tell these gags, and that takes time and care. You have to find just the right balance between capturing a child's attention through the artificiality of the 'set-up' – where you ask the question – and the clear but thrown-away punchline. If you look or sound too knowing, too smug and too artificial in the 'pay-off' line, your gag will fall flat. Practice is all: as before, watch and listen to the reaction of your audience. These gags should elicit a mix of laughter, groaning and a fair dose of incomprehension, with a few children not getting the joke at all. This enables the room to be full of people trying to pin down the gag for everyone and, ideally, many doing their best to remember the joke so that they can go off and tell someone else. As I mentioned earlier, this is the dimension within every joke, that it has the potential of 'tellability', which allows you to feel clever because you're making people laugh just by 'passing it on'.

Another thing: it's really worth trying to outsmart your audience by making up new jokes. Most of the jokes in joke books are familiar to older children. You don't want an audience full of children who can appear to be cleverer than you because they know the joke. The moment will be undermined by the wise guys saying, 'Heard it!' To win on the surprise-meter, ideally you want some fresh gags that you can be pretty sure no one in the room has ever heard before. Or at least some variations on a standard joke, which has its advantages. The benefit of using old formats is that half the joke is already told for you: the children know what to expect. Your job is to work in surprising elements within that known framework. This also enables you to use a form and disrupt the form itself. Take the knock-knock jokes, for example. There's the old one:

Knock-knock.
Who's there?
Cows.
Cows who?
No, they don't. Cows moo.

Or

> Knock-knock.
> Who's there?
> You know.
> You know who?
> No, YOU know who.

They're great, but everyone knows them. You can make up your own disrupted knock-knock jokes in a live performance.

The story-joke is also available to you. These are jokes that last longer than a quick two or three lines and which end on a punchline. Again, beware the well-known ones or you'll come a cropper because the audience will be saying the ending along with you – always a dampener! One way to get some freshness into these story-jokes is to adapt 'adult' jokes. My most successful story-joke by a mile is one that is too rude to tell children in its original form. It was told to me by a teenage girl who had just arrived from Jamaica. It involves a man who buys a horse, who doesn't know how to get the horse to go, or to stop. The man selling the horse says, to

44

get the horse to stop, you have to say, 'Whoa, Jinny!' but to get the horse to start you have to say 'Raas!' (If you know your Jamaican creole, this is a rude word.)

The man rides off and he's galloping down the road when he suddenly realises that he is coming to a huge cliff and he'll go over it unless the horse stops. Trouble is, he can't remember the words to get it to stop. The horse gallops on, and reaches the very edge of the cliff when he manages to remember what to say. He calls out, 'Whoa, Jinny!' The horse stops. To his huge relief, he lets out his favourite swear word, 'Raas!' and the horse starts up again and dives off the cliff.

End of joke.

As you can see, in this form, the joke is untellable in schools and the like. So I adapted it. I reckoned that we needed something more ridiculous and more absurd for the word the man needed to remember to get the horse to stop. I figured that that would make the children concentrate on it, and think that it was the point of the story. A good distraction. I chose 'Bellybutton!' Then, to get the horse to go, we needed something that expressed relief (so that the gag at the end of the story works) but should also be very ordinary. I chose 'Thank goodness!' To make the joke work, halfway through the story, I became the man on the horse, shouting, 'Oh no, how do I get the horse to stop?' Children, being children, shout out, 'Bellybutton!' I ignore them, the horse gallops on, the man shouts out again, 'How do I get the horse to stop?' They all shout out again, 'Bellybutton!' I 'remember' and I too shout 'Bellybutton!' The horse stops. I wipe my forehead, as if that's the end of the joke and then, still as the man, I say, 'Thank goodness!' and the horse goes over the cliff. To add to the visual aspect I act out the galloping, stopping and diving over the cliff, using my hands as the cliff and my fingers as the horse.

This is a classic 'mishap' joke, which combines all the best elements we've been exploring in children's humour: playing on the anxiety that bad stuff happens and might happen to you, on the surprising ending, on language and on the children's sense of superiority over the noodle in the story. As a joke it never fails and I hardly ever meet anyone who knows it.

This type of joke puts a lot of pressure on single words, which, to win their right to be funny, need to be surprising in some way. This can be because they are inappropriate, daft, utterly unexpected, a bit rude, a good pun and so on. Here's a classic from the old school:

Adam and Eve in the Garden of Eden
Admiring the beauties of nature.
The Devil jumped out
of a Brussels sprout
and hit 'em in the eye with a potato.

These days, many children won't know who Adam and Eve are, won't know what Eden is, won't get the double entendre of the 'beauties of nature', won't know who the Devil is, won't know why it's so inappropriate he's jumping out of a Brussels sprout or indeed hitting anyone in the eye with a potato. None of this matters. I use it a lot because the rhyme and rhythm work so well and because the last line has got the classic slapstick mess, with the little added fun that you wouldn't expect it to end with a potato. It's a good reminder for you, the joke-scholar(!), of how a really good comic poem works on each line, setting up comically inappropriate or daft situations, and then finishes with the comic, unexpected word at the very end. The tight rhythm and the more or less tight rhyming ('nature'/'potato' can work if you do it in a London accent – 'nay-cher'/'pot-ay-ter') parcels the words up in a way that satisfies the ear for symmetry and slickness.

Good comic poetry almost seems to mock that symmetry and slickness, as we saw earlier with Edward Lear, who wrote perfectly metrical, rhyming poems which seemed to imply they should be about rather grand or important things but in fact were about strange, odd, absurd people or creatures with very little purpose or very few sensible motives or outcomes – people like the Jumblies, or the Pobble with no toes. They are a bit like perfectly formed Georgian houses on the outside but inside there are no rooms, no kitchens; they are full from the ground to the roof with purple jelly and custard.

Wordplay itself – through tongue-twisters, back slang, clever-clever streams of words – may well invite awe and the desire to repeat the joke to others. When you're performing, it's a good idea to have some tongue-twisters or some back slang in your repertoire as they are great warm-ups, and really useful for gear changes and closers. I've done a whole anthology of them called *Walking the Bridge of Your Nose*. These too disrupt language by creating streams of stuff that at first are too complex and muddling to make sense, and only afterwards have real meaning. My favourite lingo is 'key jug language': spell a word out loud, saying the word 'key' after each letter, and saying 'key JUG' after the last letter. The faster you do it, the more incomprehensible and funny it becomes. Remember, children are often worried that they can't make sense of what adults are trying to say, and are often concerned that what they themselves are saying don't make sense. These tongue-twisters and word games act as relief. Even more so if you can put a stream of this together yourself and surprise another child or, better still, an adult.

Finally, don't be afraid to sing! There are a good few comic songs doing the rounds; you can find a lot of them on YouTube. I've made an album of them myself and have put them up on my YouTube channel. If you can sing (or even speak-sing) it's worth having a few of these up your sleeve. They are good for use in stories when characters need shaking or cheering up and they give the reader a moment to think both outside and inside the plot at the same time. You don't need a guitar or a piano to sing comic songs. All you need is timing, and this doesn't have to be strict musical time. This is the timing of the street balladeer of the marketplace, who calls out his song to grab people's attention. I do this one:

There was an old man
whose name was Lord Jim
He had a wife who threw tomatoes at him.
Now tomatoes are juicy
don't injure the skin.
But these ones they did,
they was inside a tin.

I do it music-hall style, as if I'm telling a story. I tell the children that a lot of what I do I owe to my dad who was a very clever man. In fact he was a professor. He taught me all sorts of things: all about William Shakespeare, and all about maths, and things like that . . . and THIS! Then I sing the song (playing with expectations, there!).

What's great about it as a song for children is that usually only half the audience 'get' it and the other half have to explain it to the others. Which makes it a good closer.

Conclusion

First and foremost, think of this business of making children laugh as deadly serious, requiring you to be a collector and student. You're a collector of anything and everything that made you laugh when you were a child. You're a student of others who make children laugh, whether that's in the distant past, or present-day writers and performers. You're also a student of 'why?'. Don't let yourself reduce your audience to 'Well, they're kids, they'll laugh at anything.' Probe why it is that a particular joke gets a particular reaction.

If you're going to do your comedy purely and simply with writing, then think of how the great comic writers build up to humorous climaxes, using tension and expectation. If you're going to use performance, think of your voice, face and body: these are the instruments that 'play' your humour just as a musician plays a guitar or piano. A look, a wiggle, an eyebrow, a moment of silence while the audience 'get' what it is you're saying, might end up being funnier than any joke. In my 'No Breathing in Class' or 'Hot Food' poems, some of my biggest laughs come because of the way I say things like 'Oh there's Melanie . . .' and – believe it or not – the way I say 'Nice!' To help you with your performances, ask yourself, 'Which actor, performer or comedian am I like?' The chances are that you'll be able to import something of that comedian's timing and look into how you do your work.

And here's one I made up earlier:

'Why was the Abominable Snowman so hopeful?'
'Because the best was Yeti to come.'